TALES
FROM THE
HAUNTED WEST

TALES
FROM THE
HAUNTED WEST

✦

WORDS AND PHOTOGRAPHS
BY E. S. KNIGHTCHILDE

KNIGHT SKY PICTURES™

ESTES PARK, COLORADO

Tales from the Haunted West

Copyright © 2023 by E. S. Knightchilde

Portions of this book were previously published, and all were revised for inclusion in this volume.

"The Letter by the Side of the Road" was first published under a different title in the February 2018 issue of *The Ghost Town Gazette* and appeared in the first edition of *Ghosts of the West: Tales and Legends from the Bonanza Trail.*

"The Mourner in the Woods" was adapted from "A Lucky Shot at Riches" and "A Lady Called Silver Heels" as published in the first edition of *Ghosts of the West: Tales and Legends from the Bonanza Trail.*

"The Uninvited" was first published in the October 2019 issue of *The Ghost Town Gazette.*

"A Shadow Where There Is No Light" was first published in the October 2018 issue of *The Ghost Town Gazette.*

First Edition

Library of Congress Control Number: 2023933525

To those who came before us,
and to those who were here before them

CONTENTS

INTRODUCTION

"Have you ever encountered a ghost?"

A test screening of *Ghosts of the West: The End of the Bonanza Trail* had just finished. Intended as a serious work on the history of the Old West's ghost towns and mining camps, the film had taken ten years to research, produce, and prepare for theatrical exhibition. After immersion in the topic for so long, I had felt prepared as I walked on stage for the Q&A after the end credits. However, I had never anticipated a question about the supernatural.

While the audience waited for an answer, the foremost thought in my mind was that I had to protect the film and the work of all who had contributed to it. Rather than muddy the waters with talk of the paranormal, I replied with a cursory "no" and maintained the focus on history by moving to the next raised hand.

However, my negative reply was somewhat disingenuous. The West *is* haunted.

✦

During the second half of the nineteenth century and the early years of the twentieth, fortune seekers swarmed over the territories of the North American continent in a fevered search for gold and silver. Where prospectors found color in paying quantities, the stampede that followed discovery could swell the confines of a nameless camp into an aspiring city seemingly overnight. However, many of those settlements did not outlast the ore that gave them birth; they died or vanished within years or even months of their founding. Residents often abandoned furnished homes and stocked businesses in their rush to some other bonanza or to return to the States.

The idealized image of a boom town's fate is one of a dusty street with weathered false front buildings and clapboard houses, all standing vacant and forlorn in an isolated place—perhaps in some mountain valley or harsh desert or far above timberline. Or it may be one with just a few inhabitants remaining—some old timers who linger, spending their final years believing that another strike was just around the corner, that the boom years would return, and the town would come roaring back.

One hundred years prior to this book's publication, that image may have been close to reality in many cases. Even fifty years ago, such locations still existed. But the decades passed; winter snows, summer rains, raging fires, heartless vandalism, and outright theft eventually reduced the ghost towns to shadows of what they once had been and sometimes to utter ruin. What remains today ranges from vacant fields to protected sites frozen in time to buildings restored or repurposed and unrecognizable as to their original design.

Who, where, when, what, why, and how. These are the currency of the historian's trade, and our descriptive language is necessarily utilitarian, despite any personal recognition of the poetry or romanticism inherent in a moment, incident, or era. And yet, many will admit that these places of the West are haunted—not necessarily by the supernatural, but by the metaphorical shadows that events and people cast across the passage of years.

James W. Marshall and Captain John Augustus Sutter, the '49ers, the Argonauts and the Go-Backs, Henry Wells and William Fargo, Wyatt Earp and Doc Holliday, Jacob Waltz and his Lost Dutchman Mine, Black Bart, Baby Doe, Silver Heels—the list goes on. Their names resound through the centuries, and their legends add to the ponderous weight of history.

Awareness of that background can have a profound effect when visiting a given location. One cannot explore the now-empty valley where Aurora, Nevada, once stood and not feel the figurative ghosts of her past. For here was a city of thousands once claimed by two states; here, Samuel Clemens came to prospect before leaving for Virginia City, the *Territorial Enterprise,* and a future as Mark Twain; here, the notorious Daly Gang committed a crime so audacious and horrific to the respectable citizenry that the latter rose against them and took matters into their own hands, passing judgment without hope of earthly appeal (and contrary to the demands of the territorial governor).

Over the last twenty-five years, my work has remained firmly in the realm of research and documentation of sites like Aurora across the Old West. My appreciation for these places, especially while in their presence, is heightened by having some knowledge of their history. But when exploring hundreds of ghost towns, it is impossible to avoid an occasional surprising—and sometimes inexplicable—experience.

From the somber to the sepulchral and, finally, to the supernatural, the small sample of encounters contained in this volume represents a partial yet complicated answer to that question posed many years ago. However, this time it is a much more truthful one:

Yes. The West is haunted. Its ghosts are all about us, and they deserve our empathy, compassion, and respect.

Golden Community Church, Golden, OR.

I.

THE LETTER
BY THE SIDE OF THE ROAD

Over the years, I have traveled tens of thousands of miles and documented hundreds of ghost towns. Sometimes drastic changes occur between trips to a site; other times, not even a blade of grass appears out of place.

On occasion, we visitors are presented with tantalizing glimpses into a moment from the lives of those who left their emotional and physical impressions behind, oftentimes without searching for them. Such was the case when I visited Golden, Oregon, to film for the next installment of *Ghosts of the West.*

The afternoon of August 6, 2014, was clear and pleasant. Utter silence reigned, and only the gentlest breeze occasionally disturbed the stillness. Just the church and general store remained, and placards relating a brief history of the location were their sole company.

While logging the details of the last shot filmed, that breeze returned, and movement on the ground some distance away caught my eye. I set the camera in the Jeep and walked over. As I approached, a sheet of paper revealed itself as the cause. Having seen so much vandalism and disrespect over the years, I assumed someone had left their trash behind. To my surprise, however, this was not litter but a carefully hand-written note held down ever so tenuously by a small stone. From the hole at the top of the paper, it seemed likely that it had been affixed to the historical marker at some point. When it had fallen or perhaps could no longer be secured, someone had placed the stone on it to keep it from blowing away. It was dated "6-2014," at least five weeks before my visit.

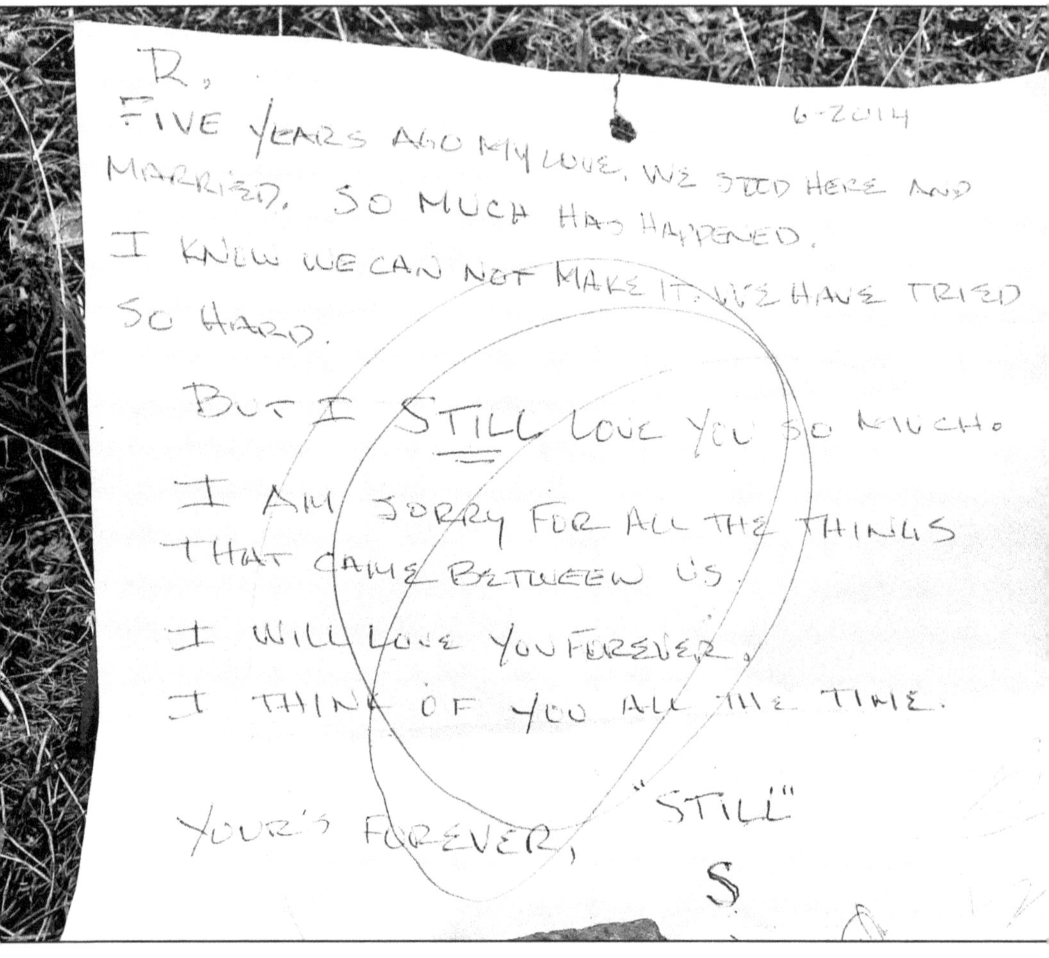

The message was brief. It was also poignant, heart-wrenching, and unlike anything I had ever seen outside the gates of a town cemetery. Was it genuine or merely the poetic expression of a recent visitor?

Belief has often exerted its hold in the years since. Against all odds, I have hoped that the intended recipient saw that note and that both have found some measure of happiness.

The note left behind in Golden, Oregon. The author unfolded the letter and shifted the rock from the center for the purposes of the photograph. The building in the upper left is Golden Community Church.

II.

THE MOURNER IN THE WOODS

While the following contains a legend held dear by many fans and aficionados of the Old West, the reader should bear in mind that there is no evidence to support its romanticized portion. Even reputable historians often overlook many contrary details and accept the unsubstantiated story as fact. [For a more in-depth look at the story using available sources from the historical record, refer to "A Lady Called Silver Heels" and "Reminiscences of Buckskin Joe" in *Ghosts of the West: Tales and Legends from the Bonanza Trail* (Knightchilde, 2019).]

According to folklore, the camp of Buckskin Joe, situated in the western portion of Kansas Territory that later became Colorado Territory, began with the accidental discovery of gold in the latter half of 1859. Joseph Higganbottam (aka Higganbotham and numerous other spelling variations, but called "Buckskin Joe" due to his choice of clothing) was out hunting when he sighted a deer or elk. Believing he had hit the animal after firing, the man searched for the blood trail. The stories do not say whether he ever caught up with his prey, but they *do* claim he found the bullet lodged in an outcrop of gold.

In its heyday, several thousand resided in the resulting boom town (or so it has been claimed), including the future Silver King, Horace Tabor, who arrived with his wife Augusta in 1861. Buckskin Joe held the Park County seat and boasted a newspaper, bank, dancing school, theaters, various stores, billiard halls, and a lively red-light district. There was also a hall where a beautiful, enigmatic young lady nicknamed Silver Heels danced.

Legend tells of a smallpox epidemic that swept the camp in the early 1860s, possibly 1861. Nearly all activity halted as residents shut themselves in, and pleas for assistance were sent as far away as Denver. The miners who succumbed lay sick and dying in their cabins; but full of compassion and unconcerned for her safety, Silver Heels visited and cared for the ill at her peril.

When the plague left the camp, the surviving miners collected a purse of $5,000 to show their gratitude, but no answer came when they called to present it at her home. Her cabin was found vacant, and she was never seen again. Some speculated that she had been stricken by the disease, and it had robbed her of her beauty. In later years, stories began circulating about a heavily veiled woman seen weeping over the graves of the miners. Yet, whenever the mourner was approached, she would dart away before anyone could catch a glimpse of her.

By 1868, the boom years had ended; the camp was nearly deserted; the Tabors had moved on to the Leadville area; and the county seat had been lost to Fairplay. It is said that Mount Silverheels, which stands to the northeast, was named in honor of the selfless dancehall girl.

Other than the cemetery and the collapsed ruins of what some believe was the dancehall where Silver Heels performed, all that now remains of the site is an empty field and a haunting legend.

The nearby town of Alma still uses and maintains the wooded burial ground. But even today, some claim to have seen the shrouded mourner in the woods, though in a less corporeal form. The apparition, dressed entirely in black, is said to vanish upon approach.

Above: Historical view of Buckskin Joe, Colorado Territory, believed to have been taken in 1864. Courtesy of Park County Local History Archives.

Below: Site of Buckskin Joe, Colorado, as it appeared in 2015.

Opposite page, top: The unpaved road leads into the cemetery (foreground) from the historical site of Buckskin Joe.

Opposite page, bottom: Burials mounds and markers for the unknown dead.

Above: Graves are scattered throughout the cemetery, many with markers that have long since succumbed to the elements or vanished altogether. In such a place, when the weather and light conspire, it is not difficult to imagine how the sightings of the mourner in black have continued across the centuries.

III.
"SLEEP ON, DEAR CHILD"

Walk through any cemetery from the mining days, and you will find evidence of the tragic, the somber, and the horrific. Though faded and weathered by time, inscriptions on markers tell of devastating grief and can yet elicit strong emotions in a visitor. The photos that follow are but a few of the many examples from across the West.

The Phelps Dodge coal-mining company town of Dawson, New Mexico, experienced one of the worst mining disasters in U.S. history on October 22, 1913. According to newspaper accounts, residents heard what sounded like a rifle shot, followed by a muffled roar, and felt a distant ground vibration. Flames then erupted from the mouth of Stag Canyon Mine No. 2's tunnel. Of the 286 men working there that day, 263 perished. Tragedy repeated on February 8, 1923, when 120 miners died in another explosion.

Above: In addition to compensating the victims' families, Phelps Dodge erected iron crosses on the graves of the deceased.

Opposite page: A reminder that each deceased miner left behind an enduring pain.

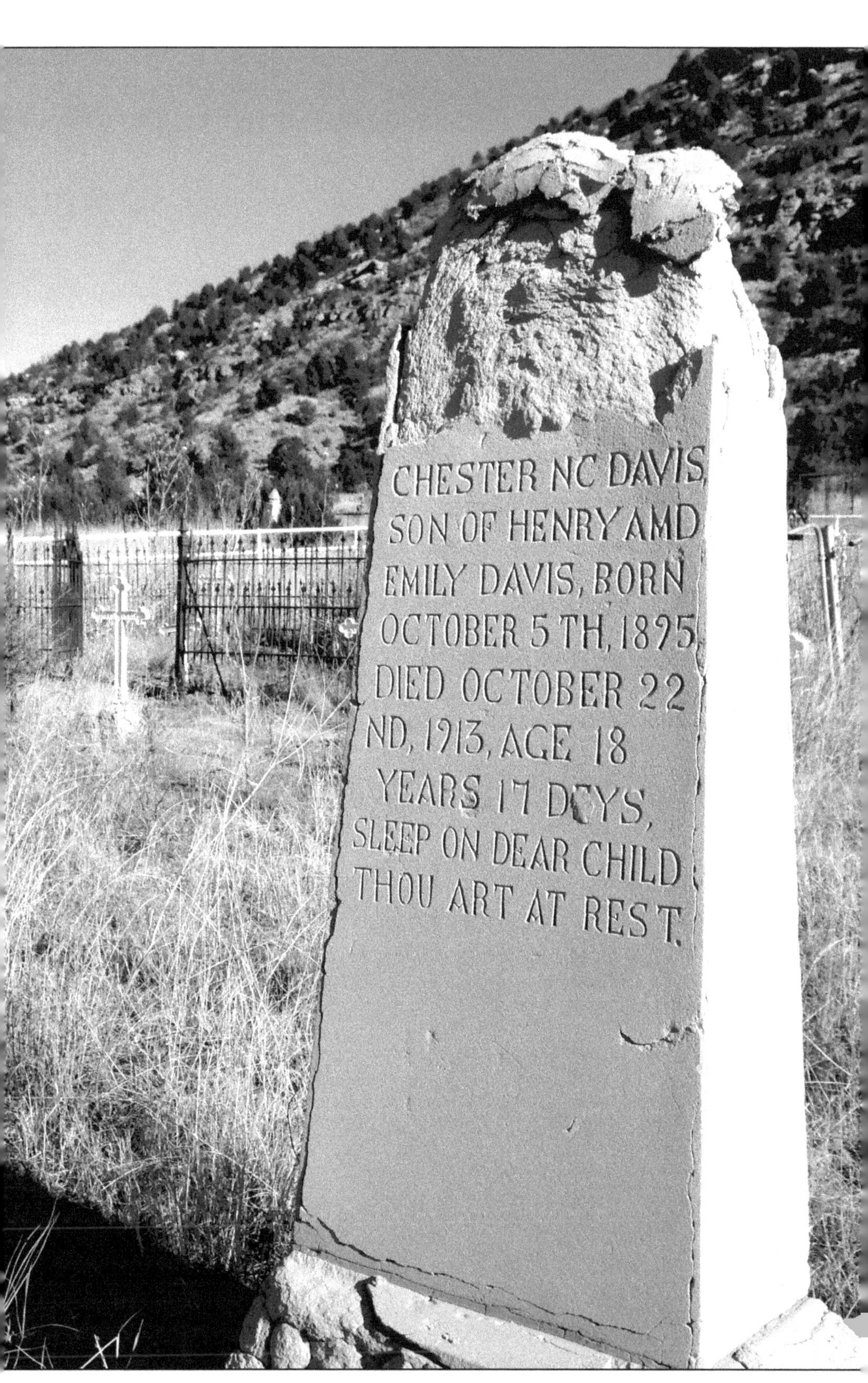
CHESTER NC DAVIS,
SON OF HENRY AMD
EMILY DAVIS, BORN
OCTOBER 5 TH, 1895,
DIED OCTOBER 22
ND, 1913, AGE 18
YEARS 17 DAYS,
SLEEP ON DEAR CHILD
THOU ART AT REST.

The magnitude of coal mining accidents was often much greater than those involving precious metals. Coal dust suspended in the air could ignite, instantly killing many in the resulting explosion. Others often perished by asphyxiation or carbon monoxide poisoning after being trapped. The mining disaster at Scofield, Utah, began with the detonation of a single black powder keg that ignited suspended coal dust, which in turn ignited many more powder kegs.

Though the death toll was eclipsed by the 1913 Dawson catastrophe, the cemetery at Scofield attests to the shattering loss of family members in a single moment.

Calamities could strike anywhere, anytime.

On Christmas Eve, 1894, in a dance hall above a Silver Lake, Oregon store, a children's pageant ended in tragedy when a lantern fell to the floor, and cotton "snow" decorations erupted into flames.

The time-scoured monument pictured below lists the names of the dead and bears the inscription: "Erected by the relatives and friends to the memory of those who lost their lives in the fire at Silver Lake, OR. December 24, 1894."

Grief etched in stone at Iron City, Colorado (above), and Elkhorn, Montana (below).

As the images on the previous page attest, stoic reminders of a painful loss that merely hint at the suffering of a dead child's parents are commonplace in the West. The photo above shows the graves of three siblings who passed away on May 23, 1884, and rest in the cemetery at Sterlingville, Oregon. Though the cause or causes of death are not revealed on the headstones, one can empathize with the unimaginable heartache borne by their father, who survived them. The inscriptions read:

AARON, Son of G & A Yaudes, Born Feb 19, 1879, Died May 23, 1884. Sheltered and safe from sorrow.
LETTIE, Dau. of G & A Yaudes, Born Dec 7, 1875, Died May 23, 1884. A little flower of love transplanted to bloom in heaven.
ALBERT, Son of G & A Yaudes, Born Dec 5, 1873, Died May 23, 1884. Asleep in Jesus blessed sleep from which none ever wake to weep. (sic)

In 1889, the father was laid to rest to the right of his eldest with the inscription:
GEO. YAUDES, Died Sep 16, 1889, Aged 65 yrs. Father let thy grace be given that we may meet in heaven.

One wonders whether the wish to meet in heaven may have been for Mr. Yaudes to reunite with his children.

THOMAS
FALEY
BORN
May 22 1853
DIED
Feb 5 1888

FALEY

Opposite page: The marker for Thomas Faley in Buckskin Joe, Colorado, reads: "Born May 22, 1853. Died Feb 5, 1888. T. Faley was lost in a snow storm while going to his mine on Feb 5, 1888 and was found June 15, 1888."

Above: On June 14, 1903, a catastrophic flash flood claimed the lives of 238 men, women, and children as it roared through and destroyed much of Heppner, Oregon, a town of about 1,300 people. Markers for entire families are located throughout the cemetery, along with a memorial, pictured above, which lists the victims' names.

The last resting place of Evelyn Myers, who died before her third birthday in Bodie, California.

One cannot consider the history of the West without acknowledging that the first Americans lived there long before the arrival of Spanish explorers or settlers from the United States.

Despite treaties recognizing the land rights of the High Plains natives, the intrusion of miners and settlers, accelerated by the 1858 gold rush to what would become Colorado Territory, led to increasing conflict with the Cheyenne and Arapaho Tribes.

Beginning near dawn on November 29, 1864, Col. John M. Chivington and the troops under his command slaughtered approximately 150 to 230 people at Sand Creek. Most were women, children, and elderly, and all believed they were under the protection of the United States. Soldiers looted and mutilated the dead, brandishing grisly "trophies" on their return to Denver.

Territorial governor John Evans, a genocidal demagogue who enabled Chivington and others like him, was forced by the federal government to resign for his part in the massacre. In 1895, the Colorado legislature renamed a 14,271-foot Front Range peak in his honor.

Today, much of the land on which the massacre occurred is protected as a National Historic Site. The closest settlement to it is still called Chivington. As of the publication date, new names are under consideration for Mount Evans.

Above: Cottonwood trees line the distant banks of Big Sandy Creek at Sand Creek Massacre National Historic Site, Colorado.

A decaying welcome sign (above) and abandoned businesses (below) in Chivington, Colorado.

IV.
THE UNINVITED

On a bright October morning, we drove south into the Bradshaw Mountains, leaving Prescott, Arizona, in our rearview mirror. Not long after descending the western slope, we turned onto an eastbound road that led into the desert; and it quickly revealed itself as the most rutted, washboard trail I had ever had the displeasure of experiencing. Speeds above ten miles per hour shook the Wrangler so violently that we imagined we were casting Jeep parts out among the saguaros. Even at a relative crawl, large dusty plumes followed in our wake, announcing our passage across the arid landscape.

About six miles after the turnoff, we pulled into an empty parking lot at the ghost town of Stanton. According to legend, Charles P. Stanton, a Machiavellian criminal who was no stranger to coercion and murder, seized control of Antelope Station in the late nineteenth century and renamed the settlement after himself. His reign of terror ended when he forced his attention upon an unfortunate Mexican girl, and her brother shot him to death in retribution. Today the Lost Dutchman's Mining Association owns the townsite, maintaining it as a recreational RV park for its members' use. [For more on this site's history, refer to "Hell with the Fires Out" in *Ghosts of the West: Tales and Legends from the Bonanza Trail* (Knightchilde, 2019).]

My partner and I walked toward three surviving buildings under roof that awaited exploration. The air was still, and only our footsteps broke the silence. Disappointment greeted us at the old hotel as an unsightly collection of chairs, junk, and staging in front rendered it unworthy of capture on film. It was also locked. We moved on to the saloon but found it had little beyond its bar to recommend it.

After the bone-jarring drive to get there, I would not leave without some photos for consolation. My partner left to continue his investigation while I set up the camera. When I finished, he was nowhere to be seen, so I headed to the last of the remaining structures. Stanton's store now served as a member check-in with a shop that offered items meant to appeal to a tourist's eyes. Inside, I found him conversing with a pleasant elder. Rather than interrupt the chat, I perused the merchandise.

A map purporting to show the locations of Arizona's lost mines immediately sparked my interest and held it—until the unmistakable sound of boots striding across a wooden boardwalk distracted me. The approach grew steadily louder, and I glanced up, fully expecting to see the door open at any moment. Instead, the footsteps passed by, and I resumed my study. Presently the visitor returned, heading back the way he had come. Again, he did not enter but continued pacing along the front of the building from one end to the other. I looked toward my partner and the caretaker. The noise had not disturbed their conversation.

I decided to buy the map as a souvenir, ending both our stay and the wait for the person outside. While attending to the purchase, I lost track of the boot steps. Upon leaving, I looked around but could find no trace of the visitor. I thought that perhaps he had taken a break from his pacing and entered the saloon, but upon glancing toward the parking lot, I saw no other vehicle but ours. Nor were there any dust clouds present to betray a sudden departure out of town on the washboard road.

My partner asked, "What are you looking for?" Perplexed, I replied, "Did you hear someone walking around out here, back and forth the whole time you were talking to that lady?" When he said he hadn't, I added, "It sounded like boots on a boardwalk." We scanned the site, and something that hitherto had escaped my notice then captured my attention. Primal instincts awoke; a cold chill traveled down my spine, and I stopped mid-stride.

"There's no one else here," I stated with quiet finality. My partner looked back in my direction, and I pointed to the concrete slab in front of the building. "And there's no wooden boardwalk to have made those sounds."

Perhaps my subconscious mind imagined it all. Or maybe I had been standing where Charles Stanton was killed so long ago, catching an echo of the last sounds that came to his ears before a gunshot ended his life— the footsteps of a man seeking to avenge his sister's honor and who perhaps still strode with grim determination on a long-vanished boardwalk.

V.

A SHADOW
WHERE THERE IS NO LIGHT

All about us are the shadows of that which came before. Whether we visit the quiet streets of Bodie or the wind-swept meadows of Buckskin Joe, the ghosts of the past are ever-present. Oftentimes, they are no more than the faintest of echoes, resounding quietly across dusty years. On rare occasions, a powerful vestige remains, a palpable remembrance of a life lived long ago yet lingering in a world that has forgotten. Perhaps it is a mischievous, childlike innocence haunting the ruin of a once happy home or a profound, overwhelming sadness—a grief that endures beyond all hope of solace.

And then there is that other kind, manifested by an isolated patch of cold air on a hot summer's day or a shadow just a bit deeper than those around it—the kind that stirs a primal sense of unease and awakens childhood fears of all that hides in the secret places of the night—the kind that walks alone in darkness and hides from mortal eyes.

✦

The early August afternoon lacked any sign of the vitality and vibrancy that was the proper domain of summer. Life and color had departed, leaving in their wake a grey quietude, like an autumn racing headlong into winter. Even the sky offered no assurance that light and heat might return: it was an October sky, cold and damp; a fog-like mist and an ever-present threat of rain wrapped the world in a dreary veil.

We looked out at the vacant field from the comfort and warmth of the Wrangler. Every book we had read stated unequivocally that no structures remained at this site. Only one sentinel stood guard over the ghost of the long-vanished town: a partially collapsed wall on a small knoll overlooking a gully. And across the field parallel to the road, the woodland engaged the heath in a struggle unseen by human eyes, its front line of trees steadily reclaiming its ancient realm. In the silence, my partner and I exchanged doubtful glances, then again considered the meadow and the inscrutable forest beyond. The woods beckoned through the mist. *Was that a cabin? Right there ~ just beyond the trees.... Or was it a trick of the dim light?*

We grabbed the film equipment, headed across the grassland, and entered the murky silence beneath the boughs. Always it seemed that a cabin hid just beyond the limits of mortal vision. After a time, I halted as my partner continued exploring ahead, and I scanned the pathless woods behind us. If we ventured further, the way out would be lost. No hints of bright sunshine would guide us back into the light, for all the land was shrouded in gloom. *We are following the call of a siren,* I thought and called out the name of my bolder companion. The timbre of my voice seemed hollow in the false gloaming, but he followed the sound and returned some moments later. We left that forest of wraiths as we had come, and the first heavy drops of cold rain fell when we stepped out from under the canopy. Had we been superstitious, we would have concluded for a surety that elemental spirits were displeased at our escape.

My partner walked back to the Jeep, but I wanted to film at least the ruined wall we had seen upon our arrival. I turned to my right and angled through the wet grass toward the center of the field. From the direction I approached, the image would lack the cinematic depth for which I hoped, so I circled to the far side that overlooked the gully. The grade would present an additional challenge, but I had come this far and would not be deterred. I moved down the wet slope, constantly looking back up the hill to see if the composition I sought could be achieved. I soon reached the bottom.

The gully curved across the field back toward the forest, and aspens had advanced along its length, forming a small copse at the broad base of the hill. I studied the shadows under the boughs. *Was that a cabin? Right there ~ just inside the grove?* A small path led the way, so I took a few steps and entered the embrace of the trees.

All sound was extinguished; a sudden cold filled the air, and I froze in my tracks. A cabin under roof rose before me—a standing structure where none should be. *And I was not alone.*

Something occupied that rotting building—something enraged by the intrusion into its decades-long sleep. Unseen, it flew across the doorless threshold, racing to cover the few paces between us. It stopped before me, close enough that I might feel its rasping breath on my skin had there been any to feel. Fear of all that lay beyond mortal harm seized and held me in its grip as the entity circled to my left, always with its gaze fixed upon me, always snarling its ethereal ire while I remained paralyzed with a racing heartbeat pounding in my ears.

Confronted by the unimaginable, my mind held tight to the familiar like a shipwrecked sailor clinging to a rock amidst a tempest-lashed sea. I shook visibly, not daring to face the thing at my side—the thing I felt rather than saw. With all the strength and courage I could muster, I whispered, *"I'm only here to take a picture."* Operating by instinct, I threw open the aperture, spun the focus to "universal," and under-cranked the camera. Somewhere in my mind, I counted off the seconds, each moment lasting an eternity. I muttered an apologetic *"thank you"* when I finished shooting and quickly headed back along the path through the trees.

Sound returned to the world as I left the grove, and the rain fell in cold, angry drops. Badly shaken, I climbed out of the gully and hurried toward the road where my partner had pulled the Jeep forward, waiting. "Where did you go?" he asked. "You just vanished."

"Drive," was all I could manage to say.

Once we were a safe distance away, I relayed my experience. My partner studied me from the corner of his eyes as he watched the road ahead. He knew I had always dismissed supernatural tales as mere campfire entertainment. But this was far outside the norm. Regardless of what had occurred when I was out of sight for those missing minutes, he could tell I believed the truth of my story without question; and I had no reason to lie.

✦

My memory from that moment until the following morning is blank with one exception: that night, a series of horrific dreams as I had never experienced before or since descended upon me, tormenting without mercy. *Disembodied, I was held captive above the ground, helplessly watching as the entity drifted from the empty doorway of the cabin and glided along the path out of the grove. It floated across the field and followed the winding, graded road we had driven when we departed.* I awoke then, heart racing, covered in sweat. I remained unmoving, terrified, a child frightened of the thing beneath the bed, believing the slightest movement would draw its attention.

In time, sleep returned. And the dream resumed where it had left off.

 Again, I awoke; again, I remained frozen in the unnatural night; again, I eventually slept; and again, the vision continued.

The clock read 3:30 AM when I woke for the last time; the thing that pursued me had covered three-quarters of the distance to where we had stopped for the night to rest. Sunrise was still hours away; I would not risk sleeping a fourth time.

Through the darkness, I waited; and when the predawn glow began seeping into the room, I woke my partner. "Let's just go. I'll drive; you can sleep in the Jeep. I need to get out of here." We loaded the Wrangler and departed as morning light crept across the landscape, returning warmth and color to the world. Before the next sunset, I would put as many miles as possible between us and that place of persistent twilight; and in the years since, I have never returned.

✦

MORE ON THE GHOST TOWNS OF THE OLD WEST

Want more ghost towns? To inquire about a lecture or screening for your group or to peruse the online store, visit KnightSkyPictures.com, or write to Knight Sky Pictures, 215 W. Riverside Dr #992, Estes Park, CO 80517. A selection of available products, with prices current as of June 2023, appears on the following pages.

Ghosts of the West: The End of the Bonanza Trail DVD

The Best Documentary Award-winning feature, presented uncut in its original theatrical aspect ratio.

Extras include approximately fifteen minutes of deleted scenes and interviews, including Disaster at Summitville, The Decline of Silver Cliff, The Lost Blue Bucket Mine, and more!

The fifty-seven-minute feature is available as a stand-alone DVD or as a DVD & CD soundtrack combo. Starting at $20.

A photo book drawing upon twenty years of research and travel to hundreds of ghost towns throughout the West.

The text is partially based on the Best Documentary Award-winning feature, the next installment currently in production, and the multimedia lecture "Ghost Towns of the American West." It also includes material that is not in the lecture or films.

The second edition includes revised text and even more photos than its predecessor, measures 6 by 9 inches, has full-color covers, and contains 128 black & white pages. The trade paperback is available as a stand-alone volume or with a special "Bodie: Then and Now" bookmark and CD soundtrack combo. Starting at $22.

The Ghost Town Tee Shirt, Colorado edition

The limited-run Ghost Town Tee Shirt features the poster art for *Ghosts of the West: The End of the Bonanza Trail* with "Colorado" in large letters above and behind a spectacular, abandoned 1880s hotel.

The dark heather tee is available in four sizes (S, M, L, XL) while supplies last. $22

Ghosts of the West Original Motion Picture Soundtrack Album CD

Looking for the perfect music to accompany your ghost town and Old West reading and exploring?

Adrian L. Hernandez's acclaimed score for *Ghosts of the West* captures the extremes of the Old West beautifully, along with the sense of nostalgia that we, generations removed, have for the era. The CD contains the entirety of the film's score, presented in its proper order, and comes in a full-color, eco-friendly, space-saving cardboard sleeve. All musicians involved would go on to perform at the 2013 Presidential Inauguration.

$11 (or at a discount as part of a book or movie combo).

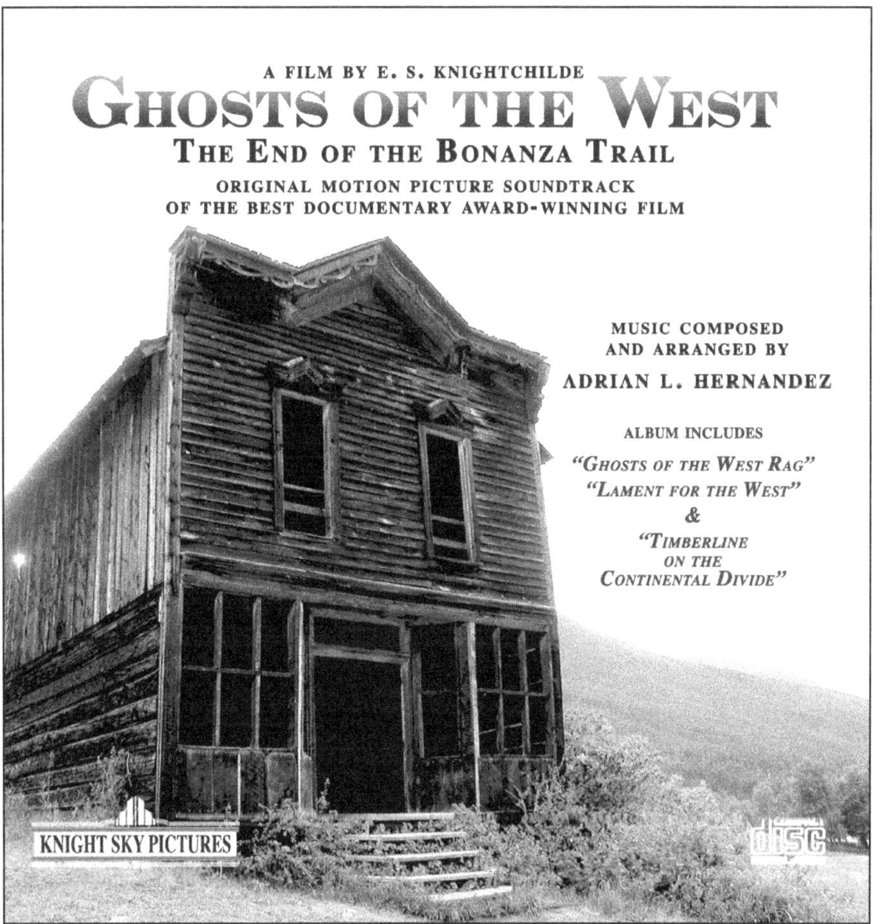

Vintage Style *"Greetings from"* Postcards

Send a postcard through time!

These cards feature a vintage look with a full-color front side. On the "Greetings from the Old West, USA" card, each letter contains an iconic image of a ghost town, mining camp, or landscape from across the western states. "Greetings from Bodie, CAL." includes photos of famous facades and interiors from the world-renowned site.

Printed on sturdy 14 pt. stock to survive mailing, the postcards measure 4.25" x 6" and feature a high gloss front that makes the art stand out with an uncoated back for ease of writing a greeting and address. Available in packages of 10 for $10.

Ghosts of the West **Production Stills** – Peruse a set of haunting images from location shooting for the first installment of *Ghosts of the West.* Color and sepia, matted and metal, signed and numbered, limited edition prints start at $29.

ABOUT THE AUTHOR

E. S. Knightchilde is the writer-director of Best Documentary Award-winner, *Ghosts of the West: The End of the Bonanza Trail,* and the multi-award-winning short, *Not for Today, But for All Time….* He has presented multimedia lectures about ghost towns to capacity crowds and is currently working on the next installment in the *Ghosts of the West* film series, subtitled *Stampede on the Bonanza Trail.*

Knightchilde has traveled tens of thousands of miles over the last two decades to film and photograph hundreds of ghost towns and mining camps of the Old West. He is a former President of the Ghost Town Club of Colorado (ghosttownclub.org) and resides in the Rocky Mountains.

E. S. Knightchilde filming for Ghosts of the West at South Park City Museum, Fairplay, Colorado. Courtesy of Karl Johnson.